TRAVIS PIANO COLLE

CW00671877

WISE PUBLICATIONS
LONDON / NEW YORK / SYDNEY / PARIS / COPENHAGEN / BERLIN / MADRID / TOKYO

Published by:
Wise Publications
8/9 Frith Street, London W1D 3JB, England.

Exclusive distributors:
Music Sales Limited
Distribution Centre, Newmarket Road,
Bury St. Edmunds Suffolk IP33 3YB, England.
Music Sales Pty Limited
120 Rothschild Avenue, Rosebery, NSW 2018, Australia.

Order No. AM976305
ISBN 0-7119-9802-7
This book © Copyright 2003 by Wise Publications.

Compiled by Nick Crispin.
Music arranged by Derek Jones.
Music Engraved by Paul Ewers Music Design.
Cover design by Fresh Lemon.
Cover photograph by Tom Sheehan.

Printed in the United Kingdom by Caligraving Limited, Thetford, Norfolk.

Your Guarantee of Quality:

As publishers, we strive to produce every book
to the highest commercial standards.

The book has been carefully designed to minimise awkward
page turns and to make playing from it a real pleasure.

Particular care has been given to specifying acid-free, neutral-sized paper made
from pulps which have not been elemental chlorine bleached.

This pulp is from farmed sustainable forests and was produced with
special regard for the environment.

Throughout, the printing and binding have been planned to ensure a sturdy,
attractive publication which should give years of enjoyment.

If your copy fails to meet our high standards, please inform us
and we will gladly replace it.

www.musicsales.com

AS YOU ARE

WORDS & MUSIC BY FRAN HEALY

1. Ev - 'ry day I wake up a - lone be - cause I'm
(2.) ev - er since I woke up I felt the net was

not like all the oth - er boys. And
lift - ing me out of the sea. And

2. And — you are, — as — you — are. —

Oh. —

Guitar

6

ev - er since___ a long___ time I felt___ the rain,____ and there was__

no dan - ger and no_____ more_____ strang -

- - - ers,_____ oh.

As

you are,_____ oh,_____ ah,_____

oh._____

oh._____

THE CAGE

WORDS & MUSIC BY FRAN HEALY

1. You broke the bread, we drank the wine.
2. You broke your word, now that's a lie.

Your lip was bleeding but it was fine.
We had a deal that you would try.

Come on inside babe, a-cross the line.
Come on inside girl, I think it's time.

COMING AROUND

WORDS & MUSIC BY FRAN HEALY

I think I see you com - ing to town,_____ hunt - ing me down_____
(% drag - ging)

bring - ing you round._____
(2° & % com - ing a - round.)

Ah._____

To Coda ⊕

16

Verse 2:

Tell me if I'm bringing you down
'Cause I was fine till you came along
You tell me that the tears of a clown, clown
That I'm confusing while abusing my mind.
So far away I wanna be
That's not as close to you and me
The things they call our destiny
Now why do you have to pick on me at all?
My walls are coming down.

Just tell me when *etc.*

DRIFTWOOD

WORDS & MUSIC BY FRAN HEALY

1. Ev - 'ry - thing is op - en,
3. Ev - 'ry where there's trou - ble,

no - thing is set in stone.
no - where's safe to go.___

Riv - ers turn___ to oc - eans,
Push - es turn___ to sho - vels,

Low is where your heart is but your heart has to grow.

Drift- ing un- der brid- ges, nev- er with the flow. And you real-

- ly did- n't think it would hap - pen, but it real-

- ly is the end of the line. So I'm sor-

FALLING DOWN

WORDS & MUSIC BY FRAN HEALY

1. You think_
(1.) _ I don't_____ know,_ and I swear_ that I do._
(2.) _ out of sorts,_____ but I know_ we'll be fine._

FOLLOW THE LIGHT

WORDS & MUSIC BY FRAN HEALY

33

FLOWERS IN THE WINDOW

WORDS & MUSIC BY FRAN HEALY

1. When I___ first held___ you I___ was cold,___
(Verses 2 & 3 see block lyrics)

Coda

Wow, look at you now,___ flow-ers in___ the win-dow. Such a
love-ly day___ and I'm glad you feel___ the same 'cause to stand up,___ out in the crowd,
you are one___ in a mil-lion and I love you so.___ Let's

1.

watch the flow-ers grow.___

2.

love you___ so. Let's watch the flow-ers___ grow.___

37

Oh, — oh.

Oh.

rit.

Let's watch the flow - ers____ grow.

Verse 2:
There is no reason to feel bad
But there are many seasons to feel glad, sad, mad
It's just a bunch of feelings that we have to hold
But I am here to help you with the load.

Wow, look at you now *etc.*

Verse 3:
So now were here and now is fine
So far away from there and there is time, time, time
To plant new seeds and watch them grow
So there'll be flowers in the window when we go.

Wow, look at us now *etc.*

THE HUMPTY DUMPTY LOVE SONG

WORDS & MUSIC BY FRAN HEALY

GOOD FEELING

WORDS & MUSIC BY FRAN HEALY

think-in' that we're one___ but we'll nev-er be the___ same.___

'Cause I got a good___ feel - ing___ that I know I'm___

___ not miss - ing,___ a - ny - thing you're___ giv - ing___ is - n't worth

this good feel - ing, yeah!___

Piano solo

48

I LOVE YOU ANYWAYS

WORDS & MUSIC BY FRAN HEALY

I know__ you'd di - sa - gree with me.__

Lyrics:
I just know you'd di-sa-gree,

but I love you a-ny-ways.

INDEFINITELY

WORDS & MUSIC BY FRAN HEALY

Now I can _____ see the light_

cir - cl - ing 'round_ your re - flec - tion.

And I'm gon - na stay here_

THE LAST LAUGH OF THE LAUGHTER

WORDS & MUSIC BY FRAN HEALY

LOVE WILL COME THROUGH

WORDS & MUSIC BY FRAN HEALY

1. If I told you a se-cret, you won't tell a soul will you hold
(2.) at the cross-roads of high roads and low roads and I

MORE THAN US

WORDS & MUSIC BY FRAN HEALY

1. (3.) More than us___ and we are them,___
   they don't___ know___ what's in their hands.
2. More than he___ and more than she,___
   they all___ sleep___ but we just dream.

It's more than you___ and it's
It's more or less___ means

73

LUV

WORDS & MUSIC BY FRAN HEALY & ADAM SEYMOUR

1. What's so wrong, why the
(2.) what's so wrong, why the

SIDE

WORDS & MUSIC BY FRAN HEALY

con pedale

1. Oh, I___

___ be-lieve___ there's some-one watch-ing ov-er you,___
(verse 2 see block lyric)

they're watch-ing ev-'ry sin-gle thing you say.

And when you die they'll set you down and take you through,

you'll re-al-ise one day, ah.

That the grass is al-ways green-er on the oth-er side, neigh-

But the grass — is al - ways green - er on the oth - er side,— neigh - bour's got a new car that you

D.S. al Coda

86

Verse 2:
We all try hard to live our lives in harmony
For fear of falling swiftly overboard
But life is both a major and minor key
Just open up the chord, ah.

The grass is always greener   *etc.*

SAFE

WORDS & MUSIC BY FRAN HEALY

1. Take all___ the goods from all___ the bads___

and tell___ the peo - ple that___ you've gone___ a - way.

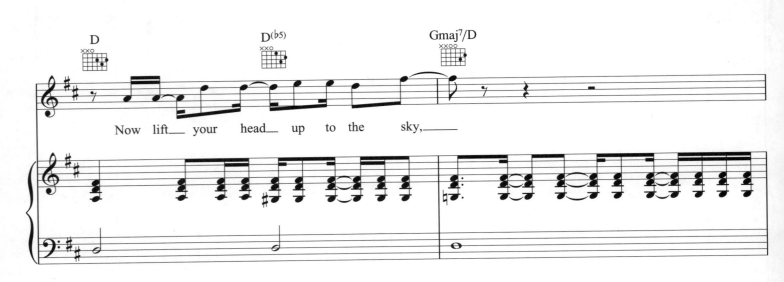

Now lift___ your head___ up to the sky,___

SING

WORDS & MUSIC BY FRAN HEALY

1. Ba - by, you've been go - in' so cra - zy, late-
(Verse 2 see block lyric)

-ly no - thin' seems to be go - in' right. So-

Verse 2:
Colder, crying over your shoulder
Hold her, tell her everything's gonna be fine
Surely you've been going too early,
Hurry, 'cause no-one's gonna be stopped now, now, now, now, now.

Not if you sing *etc.*

TURN

WORDS & MUSIC BY FRAN HEALY

the king - dom come,_____ I want to feel_____ for - ev-er young._____

I want to sing,_____ to sing my song._____

I want to live_____ in a world_____ where I be - long._____

I want to live,_____ I will sur-vive,_____ and I_____ be - lieve_____ that it won't

be ve - ry long.   If___ we

turn,___ turn,_____ turn,___ turn,___ turn.   Turn,___ turn,_____ turn.

If___ we turn, turn,_____ turn,___ turn,___ turn,_____ we might

To Coda

1. learn,_____ learn.___ **2.** learn,_____ learn.___

101

Verse 2:
So where's the stars? Up in the sky
And what's the moon? A big balloon
We'll never know unless we grow
There's so much world outside the door.

I want to sing, to sing my song
I want to live in a world where I'll be strong
I want to live, I will survive
And I believe that it won't be very long.

TIED TO THE 90'S

WORDS & MUSIC BY FRAN HEALY

like my wig___ and I hate___ my - self._____

I know it's___ all in the head._____

Hey!

Hey!

Hey! We're tired of the nine - ties._____

Hey! We're

WHY DOES IT ALWAYS RAIN ON ME?

WORDS & MUSIC BY FRAN HEALY

1.I___ can't_ sleep___ to - night,___ ev - 'ry - bo - dy's say - ing

(Verse 2 see block lyrics)

Verse 2:
I can't stand myself
I'm being held up by invisible men
Still life on a shelf when
I got my mind on something else
Sunny days, where have you gone?
I get the strangest feeling you belong.

Why does it always rain on me *etc.*

Verse 3:
As verse 1

WRITING TO REACH YOU

WORDS & MUSIC BY FRAN HEALY

1. Ev-'ry day__ I wake up and__ it's Sun-day,_____ what-
(2.) good to know that you__ are home for Christ-mas,_____ it's
3. May-be then__ to-mor-row will__ be Mon-day,_____ and what-

-ev-er's in__ my eye__ won't go_____ a-way._____ The
good to know that you__ are do-ing well._____ It's
-ev-er's in__ my eye__ should go_____ a-way._____ Still the

ra-di-o_____ is play-ing all__ the u-su-al,_____ and
good to know that you__ all know I'm hurt-ing,_____ it's
ra-di-o_____ keeps play-ing all__ the u-su-al,_____ and

what's a won-der-wall_____ a-ny-way?____
good to know I'm feel-ing not so_____ well. Be-cause my in-
what's a won-der-wall_____ a-ny-way?____

But that's not___ you.___ D'you know___ it's___ true?___   But that___ won't do.

and that___ won't___ do.___ And you know___ it's__ you___

I'm talk - ing___ to.___